# Love Speaks

## Inspirational Poetry
## from the Island of Sappho

by Frank Arjava Petter

To Madhiri     5.4. 2023

She's the One
Osho, Bhagwan, you, me
The whole ensemble
Of awakening

with love

Arjava

**Love Speaks**

1st English Edition 2021

ISBN: 9798488344051

Editor: Rosie Pearson

Layout: João Magalhães

Cover Art: Rania Dakini Salaha and Anne Schoel

Author photograph: © Karmic pro Media 2015

Typeset in Crimson Text

*Dedicated to my wife, Bhakti Georgia Mouriki*
*You are my love, my life, my inspiration*

# Table of Content

## *Love Speaks*

She sings all night and caresses the wounded hearts of the sleepers. The wind, she whispers in my ear, does not follow his own desire. He surrenders to the skies with intangible lightness and does not ask for the way. Thus he finds himself in all that is and the vastness of his heart mingles with the infinite.

# *Preface*

These texts were written between 2000 and 2020 alongside hundreds of other texts to be published at a later date. They were chosen for having a common theme, a thread that has been running through my life ever since I can remember.

They are about the only thing that is valuable in life: the love in your heart. This love belongs to no one and to all of us. We borrow it from the Universe for a while, before returning it to the Source with gratitude and humility. Love speaks to you through so many voices. Sometimes you hear her whisper in the sound of the wind passing through the trees. Another time, she awakens you with the song of a bird. She may talk to you through the words of a stranger, your Beloved, a poet or a saint. She may pierce your heart with your own voice, or with the silence that shies away from all thought and language. The use of the personal pronouns in the poetry of this volume follows the mysterious trail of the above. I, me, my, you, your, she, her, he and his are meant to point the arrow of your awareness inwards. They do not necessarily describe a person, but often a process: you.

I suggest that rather than aiming to figure out the meaning of the words, just let their melody take you to a space beyond word and meaning. Give freedom to the images created in your mind while reading: allow them to soar high and free and follow them on their flight. Forget what the author may have meant with what is being said.

This moment in which you read is all about you, dear reader: your search, your love, your life—the preciousness that is you.

# The Opening

I wonder why you ask for my hand, when it is you who holds me ever so tenderly. Do you think that I don't know, or that I may have forgotten the sacred vow?

You asked me to return when the moon is full and the tide has pulled back its velvet curtains. Thus I sit at your feet and listen to the gentle whisper of your voice.

You call me here and I follow as I always do. It is not that I can't decide for myself, but it is the sweetness in your voice that tells me that I am always in good hands when I am close to you.

# By the Light of the Moon

She sits by the light of the moon while we come and go, oblivious of her whereabouts. Rain or shine we pass by her door a Million Times, and though we long for love and its many blessings, we fail to recognize her with precision.

Her patience is exceptional and so is her attitude. She wonders who will come her way today and who will heed the call, despite our perpetual preoccupation. Yet we seek and search for her in all worldly and sacred endeavors.

Driven by pain experienced and pleasure imagined, consumed by success and disappointed by failure, we mistake her gateway for that of another, time and time again. Meanwhile she awaits our arrival as if it were for the first time.

Open your eyes, my love, she says with affection unrivaled. Her beauty radiates straight into the heart that is purified by tender awareness and unfathomable longing. It leaves you disarmed and vulnerable, ready for annihilation.

A love so deep is like a fire: wild, strong and uncontrollable. It will burn you and tear you into shreds, but know that the Whole can never be broken into pieces. It always is complete in its transcendental Oneness.

Love, she continues, is a daily death that wields the sword of dissolution of identity and fraud with kindness. Trust, she says. Let me guide you safely through the wasteland and from now on let each and every step be a homecoming.

# The Way Home

## The Harbor

Begin your journey where the open sky meets the deep blue sea. Continue onwards until the blue mingles with the children of the earth. You step ashore, and this … is your welcome.

## The Olive Groves

Caressing the surf with their gnarly fingers they stand in silence. A song of Peace is what they sing, while the audience is still busy with itself.

## The Pine Forest

Sharp needles pierce the clouds painlessly as the bees swarm out in search of the secret. But we do not speak about it in public, except in the ancient temple ahead.

## The Marsh

Sweet and salty at the same time, the ground lies low for a while. Sea or land has not been decided yet and that attracts those of us who like both.

## The Gulf

It is from here that you can see the other shore … Don't miss it. Yet you must not talk about what you see. Keep it to yourself. This is for you and your eyes. Only.

## The Orange Groves

The fragrance of the beyond intoxicates your senses, as you pass the minaret, oblivious of its existence. You don't know that this is god's country, yours and mine.

## The Wasteland

You must progress through it unhurt and knowing that at the onset of exhaustion, the weary soul deserves a rest. Exploration or withdrawal is decided in the moment.

## The Corners

The change in direction confuses the mind and gives birth to questioning. Not knowing the right way, the compass directs itself towards the source.

## The Village

Glued to the mountain-skin, held by solid rock and twisted pine, the dwellings shelter men and their companions. The longing for safety is met by the absence of danger.

## The Mountain Road

Going West, loose rocks slide off the mountain, obstructing your path. Going East, the cliff takes what belongs below with the unbearable ease of gravity.

## The Pyramids

The ancients cleared the pathway to the heavens with this in mind: life and death connected by a single thread. The choice is ultimately – yours.

## The Creek

The feast is prepared, the table set. The guests are waiting for your arrival. Temptation beckons and demands, but you must go on. It is too early to stop.

## The Moon Valley

Thus purified by the journey you encounter the mountains of the moon. They display themselves regardless of the Light. The Universe is manifest on Earth.

## The Oasis

At the edge of the moon the sunrays shyly welcome you. In their embrace, abundance shares its silent blessings, upon awakening.

# The Return to Innocence

An inkling, a scent almost intangible has been in the air for months. The senses, sharpened by years of silent observation, detect a subtle change in the atmosphere.

But what can it be that disturbs stillness without the lack of contentment? Out of the corner of the eye, I seem to see her graceful movements.

They remind me of something that I don't know. She does not allow me to breathe in her form just yet, and vanishes whenever I try.

Her fragrance intoxicates my senses ever so gently and the voice I hear makes me wonder time and again: is it her calling or is it my very own?

As a child I was told that the path was twofold, and that I could follow either one or both. A circle to be completed going East or West.

A warrior of introspection, the mind disciplined and the heart purified, I arrive at the Crossroad. Turn around, unwind my steps, the path, my life.

This is the return to Innocence, she says.

# Love Speaks

Love speaks with her familiar voice but you don't listen. You think that you have better things to do. Like a child absorbed in the most mundane of things, her voice goes by unnoticed. What is it that may attract your attention, she wonders?

She smiles and whispers, "Where are you"? You are lost in delirious daydreams. She calls your name. A slight movement—perhaps she has disturbed your slumber now? But no, you prefer to confuse yourself for now.

She tickles your soul and can't stop laughing to herself, inside. She wonders what it would take to wake you up. Seen from an outside perspective, she may seem patient, but nothing could be further from the truth.

She is free from the grip of time, unattached to the vice of judgement, unchained by the past and available to this moment. She embodies your deepest longing; she is the one you dream of every night, but still you don't recognize her presence.

She takes your hands so cautiously, then caresses your fingers with unexpected tenderness. She knows that you must wake up by yourself; the hands of another will just molest your rest. But she can't help herself. She chuckles and laughs out loud.

You look bewildered. Was it something that you heard that reminded you of a long forgotten promise? Did you give your word that you would be whole and happy, standing in your own light?

Did you promise to be well and to be filled with love and gratitude?

Did you vow that you would not hurt yourself ever again, and that you would allow love to counsel you wherever you go?

She pokes you gently and teases your senses, then pauses and leaves her efforts to the winds. It is not the right time yet. You need more dreams, more rest, more solitude before you finally – awaken.

# The First Step

We know each other casually. For weeks now I watch you pace up and down the street. Whenever our eyes meet you divert your focus. Take your time, relax.

Your fear is deeply justified. I too am certain that it would be the end. We are made for one another, you and I, and dissolution is the only consequence.

Back then we almost became one. Your hair blew in the sea's autumn wind and your voice sank deep into my heart like an anchor.

There it rests now, and even though the boat is gently rocked by the perpetual swing of the waves, it has already reached its destination.

You are waiting for my first step now, but I refrain – out of love for you. The first step belongs to you. If I take this away from you, we will walk forever in opposite directions.

# The Throne

Drowned in the deepest desperation, I sit before her throne. Forehead touching the floor, arms stretched out and hands facing upwards towards the heavens, I make my vow. Surrender or suicide, the choice is clear.

Decide, my friend, she says, and know that this is your final chance. You come and go as you wish, a Million times. But each call opens a multitude of doors which in turn exposes a Hundred and One paths.

Use the little freedom that has been granted to you in a loving way. Come with me on this journey from darkness to light and be not afraid. There is nothing to be lost and everything to be gained.

Lost and lonely and with a longing so sweet that it would burst my heart, I know what I have to do. The mirror would refuse to reflect my face tomorrow were I to decide otherwise now. Perhaps I would have thought it was my own free will.

Until today I tested your courage and your integrity, she says. I let you play and experience both pleasure and pain. Now that you must make your choice, don't hesitate. Gather courage, and leave the rest to me.

Everyone talks about me as if I were their best friend, but when I approach no one dares to speak to me. They run to the far corners to get away from me. Love, she says, is a jealous mistress: she doesn't allow anyone besides her, but herself.

Lift the veil, she says, break your masks and place all of your cards on the table, face up. Strip naked and show yourself as you are. Hold nothing back and give … give everything—less than that won't do.

My fire will consume you, she says, until there is nothing left. Let me grind you up so finely that your particles become one with the air and dissolve in the oceans. Let the Earth be the vehicle for your liberation.

And this is my promise to you: that each and every moment connects your heart to mine ever so intimately. Wherever you may be, I am. Whatever you do, it is my will. Embrace me, my love, she says, and disappear.

# All Day Long

"We are in it all day long. No matter what we do. No matter where we go, no matter where we stay. When you look up into the evening sky," she said to me, "how can you not see yourself as part of the whole … tiny, useful and unique, yet dispensable?"

I was quite surprised to hear these words from the Queen herself. Had I not imagined her to ride on the high horse of contempt? But instead, she was humble. As humble as a bee in springtime. Flitting from one flower to the next, collecting nectar and pollen, depositing both where they belong.

"You are a rose flower and I am a jasmine," she said. "Enjoy the fragrance that is yours. Do you need to ask whether or not your fragrance is to be released? Or is there a choice as to who will and who will not enjoy it?"

"But if I am what I am, how come I see something else in the mirror of my heart," I said in despair.

"You only see what you imagine to be there," she retorted.

"All you need to do is to be quiet and in that silence search your heart for its rightful owner."

I went home and opened the window. The sound of the surf carried me out onto the vast expanse of deep blue sea. There, I felt, I could lose myself. There I could feel it all around me, I could be part of it and I could see myself as merged with the whole.

But then it was time to come back. Morning broke and again the sound of the waves knocked on the window of my consciousness. Gentle, yet forceful.

And it was time to part from this place, knowing that I could not take her with me. She belonged here, with her people, with the land, the ocean and blue, blue sky. But she had awakened something in my heart, and when I sat in solitude thereafter, I would always remember what she said.

"You are a rose and I am a jasmine…"

# *Inspired by You*

You're beautiful but you don't know it yet. Your face – is written by the book of life … your life. The author keeps his character concealed in the unknown. You would not believe me if I disclosed his identity.

The many joys and sorrows shine through with intensity. You have suffered much and celebrated a little. The deserts of suffering are intervened by dry rivers of happiness.

Your features are an unsurpassed mixture of the divine play and your very own personal drama. Heart and mind are made in the image of creation. You are life itself. But tell me, what do you do with that?

While attractive both inside and out, your ignorance disturbs me a little. Have you looked into the clear blue skies lately, or are you content with the mucky places?

I see you from the corner of my eyes: you were not here yesterday. It is today that you show your uniqueness in all the colors. Covered with the mud of the past, the lotus is not soiled at all.

As it reaches the welcoming surface all pain is instantly forgotten. Giving birth to yourself is all that really matters: Time plays no part in it. This moment, I tell you, is the secret key to happiness.

# Beggar and King

You tell me that you are my prison and my liberation. I tell you that am your beggar and your king. I am free to go within your garden, but at the gate I turn and look the other way. It belongs to the past, to the days of pain and suffering.

You shower me with your flowers and wash my feet with precious perfume. You guide me when no one else is prepared to restrain my passionate nature. I sit on your throne and rule the four corners of your kingdom with love and compassion.

The seeds you sow in my heart are meant to grow protected by warm and velvety darkness. Don't consider what will become of them. Like you and like me they too follow their own path. Their destiny is unknown, their future is uncertain.

You take my hand and I hold you with utmost devotion. Your flowering is my only real concern, knowing that our scents will produce the fragrance of transcendence. Precious love, a single step will do.

# A Broken Promise

Love talks to me, but it hurts too much to hear her speak. Bruised and battered I close my house for visitors. When you walk past the tree-lined property, it all looks so perfect, but I hide inside imaginary safety, quivering. The facade is always freshly painted in happy colors. The structure appears strong and durable, the location is simply breath-taking.

She reminds me of the hard shell that I grew around my vulnerability. Her words are soft and tender; her sweet voice plucks the strings of my heart where it needs it most. The first tones are seasoned with childlike innocence. But then, when individual notes carried by an unheard rhythm join hands to become a melody, the strings of the heart tighten up.

Love and affection are my deepest longing; I seek them in the face of the unknown, in steps uncertain and dreams not yet seen. I avoid the familiar and imagine the extraordinary instead. Love unanswered and deceived are too much to bear. Loneliness has become my most cherished companion. Some are afraid of darkness while I shun the light.

Look at the immediate, she says, no matter how small. Embrace this moment with totality. This is my hideaway, the secret corner in your heart. Hold the wheel, the twig, the plow. Stop when chaos and disorder tempt you into activity. Condense awareness, slacken the cramp of constriction. Talk to me in your defenselessness, call on me in the darkest hour.

Love enters my heart in stillness. She penetrates my journey in the shy inkling of contentment. She descends on my confusion in minute fragments of surprise. She holds my hands when infinite space pervades and pulsates across the Universe.

She makes me smile when boundaries dissolve. A broken promise is the best medicine.

# *You Did Not Know Me*

You did not know then. First you walked and I sat, watching you. Then you sat while I walked. Coming closer, your eyes wide open, you did not see me. Maybe I was standing too close to you, and the fragrance of my perfume intoxicated your senses.

When you looked at me for the first time, you saw what I see when I look at you now.

Big steps and small steps, the colors of the rainbow shine through an orchestra of movement. Once in a while, you stop and say hello to someone you know. I do the same, but say nothing more, to get to know you better.

For a while we walk together hand in hand. We don't talk, but you and I know that we understand each other's silence. Once in a while our eyes meet, brushing each other's soul like young leaves in the gusts of spring.

Then we turn away, too shy to enter the sacred door – until we meet again...

# *My Companion*

I have so many friends, but you are special.

We have known each other since time began. Day after day and night after night you are here with me. Your coolness soothes my heart and the light that radiates from your being nourishes my restless soul. I cannot live without you.

All day long I feel your presence in my heart. I long for you in my dreams, and in that longing I forget myself, only to remember again when I awaken.

While dawn is parting the thick curtains of darkness, I lay awake gazing at you for hours. My hands reach out to you, but for fear to disturb your rest, I contain myself.

I know that you understand.

Sometimes your gracefulness is unbearable, and I wonder how it can be endured for one more moment. A sweet pain tears my heart into a million pieces, and I lose myself in your vastness.

When I return, you are still next to me.

I feel indebted to you for your love. I try and try again to give you something in return only to hold your emptiness in my open hands, knowing that this is how I keep the gate of my heart closed for visitors.

Tonight, I beg you for another chance...

# *Everybody's Shadow*

No one knows that I am here with you, and I like it that way.

But when the thorns pierce your skin, I wish that you knew. In those moments I hope that you would find me, even for one single second. My love would entice you, my embrace would set your heart on fire. All the birds would come home in an instant.

But you don't know me, even though I am always here with you.

I cry your tears, I laugh your laughs. I hold your belly at birth and your head when you depart. I dream of you at night and I awaken in your arms every morning. One day you will find me. On that day, the ferry-man will lean on his oars, and smile.

# *Welcome*

You are welcome, she said to me. In my harbor I keep a special mooring just for you. While the waves play with the sea and the winds blow from here to there, I wait patiently for your return. In my heart you are always here with me.

Knowing that only the one who has gone away can ever come back to me, I bless the days and bow my head before the nights in gratitude. I calculate the movement of the stars: your safety is my certainty and your happiness is my reward.

You are a blessing, she declared. The flame in your heart ignites the lover's dance, and sets his movements on fire. His longing for celebration and your contentment stage the playground for the miraculous.

You are welcome, she said to me. Under my skies there is shelter for your tears and for your laughter. While sunny days and rainy skies chase each other's shadows, I look into your eyes and see my own reflection.

# The Call for Prayer

Next time you hear the call for prayer, know that I am already here with you. Your beckoning voice cannot deceive me, for I have been in your cup all day long. Whenever you bring it to your lips, remember me, and know that with each and every sip you fulfill your destiny.

You set out to look for me in the most faraway places. You cry and cringe and try to get away. You seek the four corners of the world in agony, though in your heart you know that I am always here – with you. I understand your pain, for I, myself, am the greatest pretender.

It was I who sent you on your journey, but now I regret to have misguided you. The flower of appreciation grows in equal measure with the devastation of loss. Knowing this, I lead you in the wrong direction, hoping that you would not obey my order.

Now I beg you to return.

# A Cloudy Night

I won't ask you to stay with me tonight: it is a cloudy night. The moon lights the pathway to my heart, but the way back is uncertain. Clouds may gather later on, and you may lose your way in the dark of night.

I ask you to leave at dusk to make it easier for both of us.

My heart aches with an unknown sweetness as you walk away into the approaching night. The fragrance of your presence intoxicates my spirit and I know that it will stay with me.

I promise to visit you in my dreams, tonight.

It hurts to see you go like this. All night long I feel your body next to mine, knowing that you are far away. I feel your breath caress each pore of my skin, and your fragrance wraps me in the perfume of the soul.

You have pierced my skin. It cannot be washed away, again. It lingers in my heart and soul. It vibrates in the space that separates us, filling a thousand miles with love and ecstasy. With every breath I breathe you and more you, until I am too drunk to stay awake.

In my dreams it is easier: Both you and I disappear in the vastness and I make the bed for you where pain and pleasure meet on equal terms. Before daybreak I awake alone, feeling your presence fill the room.

It hurts to let you go and I hold you to my heart with all my might. You slip through my wanting hands until nothing remains but the waves beating against the shore with their rhythmic breath.

The waning moon does not light the last hours too well. The occasional shooting star in the Eastern Skies carries my longing back to you.

I must leave now. As I glide past the sentries of dawn, your land and your people, your love and your suffering become mine. My heart is heavy with a honey so sweet that it sticks to my soul for the remainder of the journey.

Still your hand rests on my heart, today.

# The Embrace

Don't resist my embrace today – it is a special day. Though I know that I will return to you, I hesitate to go before you have answered my call. You think that eternity is your playground and that you can postpone our meeting for another day. But another day is always now, and tomorrow hides in the secret chamber of today.

Your own desire is tiresome; it keeps you away from me, because you know what I know. You know that there is no way to avoid your own liberation, and you know that it is your own hand that hurts you so deeply. The wings of freedom are already spread in anticipation, and the wind is blowing in the right direction.

Your resistance, you think, is your greatest treasure. You hold onto it with all of your might and you defend it with a bleeding heart. Today I ask you to surrender what you will never need again: I am asking for a single breath to melt in my embrace. It is a special day today.

# *The Poetry of the Moment*

Recite the poetry of the moment, she said, and listen attentively as you speak. Lightning silence in between each syllable cracks the internal sky wide open.

There, for a moment or two, just before thunder rumbles and wind picks up, you enter the hidden sanctum. But beware as you step into the void.

The road ahead is dressed in an unfamiliar coat. The abyss behind you beckons with the bitter promise of unconsciousness.

Try to cling and be certain of a loss much more painful than you can ever imagine. Attempt to forget and it will haunt you even in your dreams.

Once you have tasted the nectar of the present nothing else will ever satisfy you. My friend, she said, recite the poetry of the moment and be free.

# A Love Long Lost

The next time we met, she said to me: "It does not make any difference, whether your heart holds onto a love long lost or a love newly gained. You are a slave in the garden of delight and a pawn in the fiery chamber of hell. Your heart is a prison, and until you find out that you yourself are the warden as well, there is no hope for liberation."

I did not know what to make of it and went on my way. I fell in love with a woman of the old country and later with one of the countries on the opposite site of Earth.

In between those worlds I saw many rose gardens. I saw rivers of gold and skies purple as nothing on earth can ever be.

Then, one day, I remembered the conversation we had and I broke free.

Two years I sat in silence in a cave in the mountains. I did not eat, drink or breathe. I did not think of the past and brood over the future. There was no light, and without it, darkness disappeared as well.

Then it was time to go back into the world of men. The shadows overpowered me at first, but after a while I learned to play the game, again. Once more I remembered her words, and decided that I must find her.

But how can you find what you have never lost?

She appeared one day, as beautiful as ever, and I swear she did not age, though I had finally matured.

"My friend" she said, "it is time for me to leave you now, because the light on the Western horizon is nearly extinct, and I must go back to my people."

"But what about me, I exclaimed in despair. "For me you are the light that lights the path. Without you, I too will wither like the morning glory in the midday sun."

"But like it," she replied with eyes that looked past the thorns in my heart, "you will arise again in the morning and see what you have missed before, with new eyes like the morning dew."

With these words she disappeared, leaving me once more. And even though I know that she is gone now, I understand that in my heart, the memory of her lives on. Until we meet again.

# The Recognition

Your visits are engrained in my memory like no other. You dress in many colors, and it is always challenging to recognize you at first. But then I see the old familiar smile and laugh with you for a while. You have fooled me once again.

It never occurs to me to be shy or to cover my pleasure with velvet curtains in your presence. I enjoy the fact that you come and go in your own rhythm, and that it seems impossible to tempt you in any way. You are at home and home remains where it is.

Yet sometimes I miss you and I drown my desire in a pool of deepening Silence. Still I hesitate to take the last step, because our unity means that I will never be able to find you again. Thus I come up to the surface again, refreshed and longing for another Visit.

# *Eressos*

Now I know why I love you so much.

You are her body, so wild and passionate. Your nakedness is all there is, intoxicating the senses. The seasons cover themselves with a dry leaf, shy of your overwhelming beauty.

You are her mind, so unpredictable and free. You challenge the conditioned with your spaciousness. The discipline of transcendence bows before you, for showing her the way.

You are her heart, so tender and true. Your children are proud to call you – mother. Love's longing is to be in your arms when all nectar has been tasted and all songs have been sung devotedly.

# This Game of Love

The opposite of love, she said to me, is love. Like a rainbow, she wears all the colors. Perhaps this is what keeps the atoms together, dancing to the tune of tenderness in unison. Listen carefully, she continued. For this does not match the experience of the many.

Love is the ultimate trickster, she said. Disguised as clown, henchman, lover and a sacred absence, she may seem like a game, a hunt, a romance or a silent moment. She masquerades her hidden splendor with encrypted activity, knowing well that her charms are irresistible.

## The Game

Pulled by the invisible strings of nature, love comes and goes at its own pace. Biological compatibility has a beauty of its own, but its expiration date is already fixed before the lovers meet. Falling in and out of love they think that this love belongs to their own hearts. This is the common playground of lust and violence—if the lovers are left to their own devices.

## The Hunt

The beach of kindness stretches forth beyond imagination, while the fragrance of convenience permeates the thick jungle of reason. In the absence of light, the sweet longing of the heart is seldom heard. Lonely together, the flower of honesty yearns for the nectar of the sun, but can't reach it. The hunters in this art run along age-old tracks, following the familiar scent, returning again and again into the welcoming arms of the known. They find the same treasure, time and time again,

infatuated with the illusion of their glorious success.

## *Romance*

Romantic love draws the curtains apart a little further, but the veil is still in place. It intoxicates the senses, but that too sticks like a small splinter in the incomprehensible mosaic of the universal heart. The object of love is lifted onto an artfully designed stage of make-believe, a dream coated in the garments of desire.

Let the sacred string in your heart be touched, she continued.

## A Silent Moment

Eternity is awakened by the silence of the desert night; it is caressed by the darkness of the clouds that hide the moon. You find it in your lover's embrace or in the innocent eyes of your child. It may find its way to you through any of the senses, or you may perceive it through the smile on the Buddha's lips.

This is the door – now enter infinite space. Real love, she said, begins in your own heart.

## The Gamble

You gamble your love away so carelessly, thinking that it is yours to do with as you please. But let me tell you this: your love belongs to me. Your heartbeat pulsates in my veins; your words are voiced and heard by my ears alone. Your body and your mind, your past and your future is not for you to play with.

Roll the dice, my friend. Sweet are your dreams and intoxicating the illusion that your chances are even. Fifty-fifty you think it is: black or white. But the dice are loaded by the twisted actions of your past and what you judge as lucid achievement is determined by your own unconscious desires. You think that you are, but you have not started living yet.

Just one more game, you think. It is time to persuade the movement of the stars in your favor. Yet the stars listen to no one, and the heavens dance in a rhythm entirely of their own making. How exhilarating is the illusion of knowing: you stand up and sit down, thinking that it is you who moves the invisible strings of your life.

I will let you dangle in suspense for another moment, my friend. Imagination is a potent sleeping pill: it beckons with the delightful honey of self-deceit. Illumination, you think, is

when all your worries disappear. But waking up is painful and the shattering of dreams leaves you broken-hearted and homeless.

Someday you must pass through it, nevertheless. No one other than you yourself can rescue you from your unconsciousness.

You will ask for it yourself when the time is ripe, when everything else has lost its meaning. Till then, enjoy and play the game of wakefulness and sleep until you have had enough. Then, come home, and wake up – smiling.

# *The Invitation*

Talk to me. Old or young, cat or dog, stick or stone. I speak your language, my friend. Briskly responsive or doomed to motionlessness, you have my undivided attention.

Your voice might be powerful or restrained, your intonation clear or faint. Your words, simple or eloquent, will find me wherever you may be. Trust your innermost wisdom.

Surprise me with your call, the gentle rustle of the leaves, the timeless whisper of the ocean, the mischievous bite of a sandstorm. Gather courage, be assured and speak.

Astonish me with loving kindness and joyful creativity. Approach with caution, greet me with certainty. Touch with love, embrace me with desperation. Have faith in the unconscious.

Charm me with your gestures, delight me with your stillness. Dance with uncertainty, sing with all your passion. Share your ecstasy, present me with your agony. Dissolve in generosity.

Talk to me in your very own way. Occupy the space in my heart: take what you need and give what you have. Then leave or stay forever. This, is my invitation.

# The Promise

I have been to your house a million times, yet I fail to recognize you every time we meet. Your fragrance should remind me, but for reasons beyond my comprehension, my senses are blocked in your presence. You marvel at my inability, but let me tell you this:

Your heart and mine are one from the moment we first met. But I have vowed not to lock the door of your palace behind me, because of a promise made a long time ago.

My ways may seem unusual, yet I am your faithful agent. I work for you by taking care of others. I carry what is theirs, and what is mine is theirs to take. They need my hand in order to find yours. I take you with me there, for they don't know how to find you.

Please do not mind if I will never stay for dinner. I must not quench my thirst, nor satisfy my hunger. The longings of my heart require a bitter medicine, while in your arms the sweetness may deter the soaring spirit from coming back again, another time.

## An Open Door

An open door, she said to me, loves everyone who passes through it, regardless. It empties itself so totally that whatever is carried by the wind is received with gratitude. A speck of dust, a grain of sand, an autumn leaf or a visit by a loved one makes no difference to its silent composure.

You may think that it has no mind of its own and you are right. You may assume that having nothing is the attitude of poverty, but you are entirely wrong. The door knows not what is to be found behind its own invitation, while it holds the secret key to liberate whosoever takes a single step beyond the threshold.

# An Open Window

Look out from within, she continued, and admire the miraculous unfolding. Then look in from without and adore the silent revelation. The one who sees it all is one and the same.

Peaks and Valleys in the faraway distance are but reflections of your own inner world. Look for beauty and love, and you will find it, surrounding you. Treasure and pluck the fruits of your love.

The shape of the land and the depth of the sea beckon you to come close. Touch me, caress me, they whisper, be the one and only one – for me. I am here for you, I am your pathway and your destiny.

Look into the silent waters and behold your own face they seem to say. Smile, as if your life depends upon it. Gaze in awe at the benevolent face of the creator, and there discover your very own image.

A gentle touch of the shoulder, the fragrance of a sweet breath, an inkling of an unknown presence and a gesture of balance are the silent messengers of the unknown. Listen to their message, my friend.

# *Kalloni*

She takes me on this road again and again and I wonder why she thinks that I need so much practice. We both know that her insistence is in my best interest. She likes to play, and so do I. Her excuses are many-faceted—one day, the supermarket; one day, the dry cleaner. The mechanic and the boutique, the hairdresser and the hardware store request my presence … now. Every inch of the way she talks to me with the intimacy of an old friend.

Those who come here for the first time are overwhelmed by the scenery. They hear her words resonate deeply within their chest and mistake them for their own voice. Oblivious of their surroundings the locals bide their time by speeding along blind corners and unseen beauty. Forever-gaping potholes and lonely donkeys share their moments with herds of renegade sheep while inches turn into miles and miles into a destination, still to be reached.

Some of my friends are bored with the inevitable, while others are irritated by their own perpetual impatience. But the journey is merciless, there is no escape. As if by divine providence, the mountains and the sea take turns hugging the trail ever so tightly, then giving it slack when you least expect it. Divided by olive groves and pine forests, the Gulf shimmers in the distance, beckoning. All the while her sole concern is with matters of the heart. It is here that I learn the art of love.

## The Secret of the Wind

Whispering, shouting speaking in tongues, howling with deafening silence, and then conversing freely – this is the secret of the wind. We hear and listen more or less attentively. We laugh and sigh, eavesdropping as we chatter along with the mystery. Is he really speaking to me or is it just my imagination?

Foraging through the jungle, accelerating across the plains, then whistling past mountain peaks and exhaling over the waves of his own making, the wind speaks all the languages. He declares and drawls, he argues and canonizes. He converses playfully with those who listen and talks gently to their hearts.

But those who resist, who cringe and struggle, and those who campaign against his voice are bound to be cut by the sharpness of his breath. They are likely to be felled by either gust or stamina, by the strength of his call and the absence of weakness. They must bow and surrender for their own good.

My friend, she said, listen to the wind.

# Your Message

What is it that you are saying to me so silently? So many different voices speak in my aching heart that I cannot make out their significance. Your loose garment of silence covers my busy overcoat of thought. Still I don't quite comprehend the language of the lover's heart.

Loud and clear I hear your voice today, but I refuse to listen. We unite in this and we separate in that. On another occasion I praise and worship you, only to find you gone. Your absence both poisons and nurtures me playfully. This is how I silently sustain myself.

Your voice is planted ever so deeply in the heart. The art of whispering the sacred name is learned in the midst of turmoil and despair. The dream of awakening shatters the mirror into a thousand triangles. Piece by piece a new image reveals itself.

Once more it is your message that I hear. Listening with quiet inspiration, each syllable, each silent intonation reverberates in sacred rooms of joyful transformation. You give me space and offer revelation. Your freedom gives birth to my responsibility.

Beloved, give me words to capture this silence. Dance me to the moon in deep embrace to understand this stillness. Offer me dreams, my love, to find awakening. Beloved, give me what belongs to no one and keep what is entirely your own. Before I find myself in you.

# The Meeting

We sit together every day. Once in a while you look at me and smile. We don't disturb the silent conversation of the hills and the joyful songs of the birds. We know about the shyness of the quiet creatures.

Under the trees, the sunlight is filtered naturally as olive leaves protect our skin from the scorching sun. They share their wisdom with the wind that carries their fragrance to the valley below.

I like it here and so do you. In your presence relaxation comes naturally. In the afternoon, when our silent work is done, we walk down towards the sea to meet the others, whose minds are filled with a thousand and one things.

You encourage them to surrender their burdens to the blue waters. You tell them that they will soon sink down to the bottom, like the pebbles that protect the beach from moving out to sea.

Some try and others do what you suggest. The other half nods their heads in agreement and does absolutely nothing. The constant chatter in their mind prevents them from engaging in their own awakening.

But you don't mind and neither do I. After sundown, we make our way to our silent quarters where nothing is said and everything is heard. We lie by the fire, arm in arm, and sleep...

# The Love for All Things

Impress me with the love of all things, she said to me. Make space in your heart, expand and welcome the guest. You are an invitation, an open door, a promise, a temptation for the infinite.

Fear not the emptiness – give love the space to occupy every nook and corner of your life. Read the poetry of the moment, sing the hymn of silence in between the rhythm of your actions.

Walk through each moment as if you were treading on holy ground. Step lightly, dance swiftly, run with confidence and stop gracefully. Be concerned with the immediate, forget this and disregard that.

Talk to me in the mountains and rivers, the trees and meadows. Embrace me in your friend, your lover and your children. Listen to me in the voices of the ancestors. Drink me

in your beverages and breathe me into your lungs.

Be a lotus petal, opening. A ripple in the pond, increasing. A footprint in the sand, inspiring. A warm embrace, welcoming. A flash of lightning, illuminating.

Be your Self, my love, she said. Nothing else is worth living for.

# *Tenderness*

Tenderness speaks softly to the rocks and flowers—I am here for you, my friend, she says. Footsteps imprinted on holy ground, the weight of the body steps onto itself. What is the self, other than a small part of this celestial body? The world is you and you are the world.

She touches the steering wheel with the same love that caresses the beloved. Identity crumbles as plastic and leather melt into the warmth of her gentle hands. Streams and meadows rush by, a flock of geese on their way South. Everything moves while spirit remains still.

All the while she whispers words of reassurance to her children – Come close to me, my love, I am your harbor, your happiness, your destiny. She knows that we don't deserve her love just yet. But still, the soft touch of her lips leave the promise of tenderness, lingering…

# My World

Let me introduce you to my world, your world, your life, she said. The door is always open, the curtains drawn back. Transparent as the clear blue skies after a heavy rain, I am here for you. I am love, I am spirit, I am everything that you are looking for.

Let this be our sacred game: In the morning in the mirror, I look straight at your face, while you rub your eyes in disbelief. You long for me as I smile at you with every moment. I find you while you look for me in all the corners of your Universe.

During the day, we continue our game of hide and seek. I like to surprise you, but you are unpredictable. Wherever I appear you are already there. You never tire of this play—you close the curtains with anticipation ... and dream of a new beginning.

At night you sigh, thinking that you can finally get away from me. You don't realize that I sit by your side and whisper sweet words of wisdom in your ears until the early morning. When you awake, alert and well-rested, the never-ending drama begins anew.

Day in and day out I attempt the impossible, while you patiently misunderstand me. But you are my sole purpose and my only pleasure in life. Without you, I would not even be, here.

# Temperature

She warms me, ever since I can remember. As a child no opportunity of her presence was left unanswered. With time and geographical adjustments her companionship became ambiguous.

Her generosity is infinite. I used to talk to her and I still do. Every cell of my being, my skin, my lungs, my heart and mind thrive on her selfless offerings. She never asks for anything in return.

She is the undisputed queen of the seasons. This makes her proximity unbearable in one moment, and the object of the most intense desire in the next. She satisfies everyone, unintentionally.

Neither critique nor longing concern her at all. She is what she is, and when. Those who love her are thrilled by this uncommon ingenuity, but find it challenging to endure it for long. She can never be owned.

She navigates playfully through periods of movement and rejuvenation. Riding the waves skillfully just now, the next instant may find her resting by the light of the moon. She follows the natural order.

At times, the nearness of her is as close as can be. At other times it appears light-years away. Like no other, she makes it so easy for us to receive: whatever destination is reached, whatever journey is underway, she is already there.

# *Invisible*

Sometimes I am invisible and no one can see me except you. This does not bother my heart most of the time, because it is only your presence that I seek. But when you hide from my sight for more time than I can bear, it hurts to be alone.

Over the years I have become so different from the others. It is not that I want to be so; it happens quite naturally. Praise and criticism don't change the tuning of the instrument; success and failure show themselves as the poles on the same spectrum.

I share the same afflictions and the same virtues as everyone, knowing that nothing exists that is strictly personal. Yet it is a lonely world in which I search for utmost honesty in everything I do and in everyone I meet.

# The Admission

"Come in, my love," she said, with a smile that embraced my heart like the first rays of sunlight that melt the morning dew. It was natural to enter with a bow, resistance out of the question. Forehead kissing the Earth, hands outstretched upwards, eyes closed tenderly: this is how you are ushered in.

The iron gate, wide open, does not make a sound. Standing in the middle of nowhere it welcomes all visitors no matter if they come or go. Footprints on gravel fade into the past while she sways softly in the morning breeze. "The price of admission," she says, "is not at all what you expect it to be."

"She will demand my life," I thought, "and ask me to sacrifice what is most dear to me. She will take my love, my heart, my truth, my bliss and my beauty." A shiver, an electric current, a sudden frost, a bolt of lightning blinded my soul with fearful anticipation. How can I say no, how can my answer be ... a yes?

I do not see it coming and have no time to prepare for her preposterous proposal. "My love," she says, "all I ask of you is that you leave behind what was never yours, and claim what has always been the open secret of your heart. Your wealth or your poverty are none of my concern.

Unload your many sorrows at the gate and walk. Surrender your pain as you step across the threshold; drop the whole weight of your suffering in this instant, and dance freely. Abandon whatever hurts your heart in this instant. Let go of the petty self with gratitude and stand in your own light.

"My love," she says, "be free."

# *Knowing*

I know that you are here with me, but you like to tease me. You hide like the blue sky behind a motionless cloud and play seek and you shall find. But you don't want to let me catch you today—I can feel it in the atmosphere.

Maybe tomorrow will be a better day for us, or the day after. Thus I practice patience – and so do you. You once told me that I must forget you completely, to prepare myself for our next meeting. But how can I forget the longing of the lover's heart?

And so we continue our game. You—from your hiding place—and I—seeking and searching everywhere. This … makes us complimentary … and this … unites us in wholeness. For without you, I would have lost my way, and without me, you would not be here at all...

# Stand Up Straight

Stand up straight, she said to me. Stretch your back, straighten your neck and breathe deeply. Stand in your own light and know that this light is neither yours nor mine.

After a long rest, my stiff muscles relax in the early morning sun. Surrounded by stillness, the movement of random thoughts is sluggish. This is the right time to awaken.

Her words have an unknown urgency that jolts me out of my heavenly slumber. Why now, I wonder, while immersed in sweetness? A few minutes, and I'll be with you.

When the etheric bodies have not quite arrived yet after a night on the town, the soul shines forth in purity. It talks to you, she says. Please listen, and listen carefully.

The right time is when your guard is low. Expectation is the servant of procrastination while practice is the master for moments of uncertainty.

What do you want? she asks me. The worldly goods I grant you if you wish. Power, greed and money are at my command. But if you long for silence and compassion, you must cease to exist.

Imagine that you are dead, she says. Everything that you think of as yours belongs to me. All else is meaningless. Sign on a blank contract and give me the deed to your life. Surrender!

# All Night

I am waiting for you all night, while you are fast asleep. Your breath reminds me of your presence once in a while. Then I suspect that there is a flame of awareness that lights the inner mansion with a soft, guiding light. But it is lit in a faraway corner of your mind and you will notice it when I am far away.

The night is clear and quiet and the children are dreaming of each other. They play hide and seek all day and continue with their game at night. Lost in bliss, they rest well as they prepare themselves for the next day. I myself am sitting by your side, your hand in mine. You wonder if I mind my night-watch, but I like it this way.

In the morning when you awake, I steal away, exactly in the right moment. I make sure that you sense my presence out of the corner of your eye. Sometimes you turn to me ever so slightly in your sleep. Still you fail to catch me ... yet. I open the door and slip out onto the street, unseen, like a thief in the night, and enter it again when you retire.

This is the game we play in all seriousness and I wonder if you know how much I love you. You may feel that I abandon you, when in fact I am with you most intensely when you are not here.

# A Ripple in the Lotus Pond

Everyone has gone to sleep, except for the frogs and the silence in between their calls. They always talk to me, as I speak with them.

Together, we watch the lotus that grows amongst them, opening. Petal by petal stretches forth in the moonlight. They know and I know. We have seen it happen many times before.

Clouds obscure the scene with their winter coats, hiding, then revealing, mercilessly. Known and unknown sounds are carried by the cool fragrance of January. In the distance, an owl flies by, unseen.

Soft, dark and muddy, the bottom of the pond thinks of itself as the whole world.

Pushing through is no easy task. The sap of life flows into one petal at a time, excruciatingly slow. The plant quivers ... this way ... and that way, ready to sink back to the bottom one more time. The gentle wind whispers in my ear, "My love, the dawn is near."

The pond takes another breath as one more petal blooms where there was darkness a moment ago. Soon they will stand before it in awe and their hearts will be filled with bliss. They will pray to the Heavens and bow deeply to the Earth. It is good that they have never seen what I see.

I get up and go home, knowing that it will continue without me. A tear of gratitude slides out of my left eye: a ripple in the lotus pond.

# *Sleepless*

I cannot sleep without you, my love—the pillows remind me of you. Almost every night I get lost in irrational dreams. Missing you is the theme I work on all night and in the morning I awake tired and never really rested. Something in me does not relax without you. It is difficult to explain because all the realms of sleep seem to be present.

I fall asleep easily and don't awaken during the night. But a deep and tender longing keeps me from dissolving into the night. It is not my work that tires me when I am abroad – it is your absence. Imagine that you have lost your way, your god, your faith, and you know what I feel when I'm away.

During the day, the busyness prevents me from realizing what is going on, but at night there is no escape. As darkness envelopes me kindly, your absence strips me of everything that I have got. It leaves me with a restlessness that is difficult to bear. Like a low fever it wears out heart and mind, one night at a time.

It is time to come home.

# Dreaming of You

I wake up in the middle of the night, dreaming of you. You are here, lying right next to me. I feel the closeness of your body like a promise of the long forgotten past.

For eternity I lay awake, dreaming of how it would be, to be with you again. We were apart for so long. Even though I hear your calming breath and see your sweet smile, you are so far away.

I am paralyzed with fear and I don't understand why it is so hard to reach out to you. I sit up and close my eyes, as I do every morning. Just one more day, I think, and I get up.

I am alone with this longing in my heart. In your sleep, you may feel the strength of my hand that could simply touch you, but it won't.

Long ago we embraced and held each other, intoxicated with the wine of innocence. So long that we looked into each other's eyes with a love so pure that the gods felt ashamed for their own crudeness.

Deep down, I do remember it well.

I am afraid to ask you for your love, which I know you would give to me so willingly. I torment my heart, day in and day out, knowing that you are here with me, while I am dreaming of you…

# The Sea (That is You)

It has become difficult to be without you. You wash away my sorrows, wave after wave. You cleanse me with your innocence, and bathe me with love and devotion. Ripple upon ripple touching the other shore, and … this one.

Your vastness is like nectar, sweet and savory. Rock becomes sand, sand becomes timelessness in your hands. Whatever is offered at your shore, you embrace. You enfold my island with unconditional tenderness. A gentle touch, a silken kiss, there!

When I am away I long for the blue luminance – the promise of the horizon meeting your skin, and mine. Your fragrance drifts past this yearning, touching it softly yet with a certainty beyond words. The look on your face imprinted in my heart, always.

This taste, this kindness knows not substitute. Once tasted it can never be forgotten. It erases both desire and memory and just – is. What lingers on is all encompassing love – permeation. Melting, merging, we swim in each other's presence.

Grace descends on unseen wings, and with hands folded in gratitude she whispers so carefully, "Never think of you and me as Two. Surrender separation, renounce duality, dismiss division and dive into the formless where you enter, Love.

# Thundering Silence

Thundering silence cracks the skull wide open. "I am yours," she says as she enters and pervades the lover's heart. Purified by the seasons, spiced with innocence, relaxation and simplicity, the heart welcomes infinity to take its rightful place.

The inner space expands like a womb blessed with a growing child. It pulsates ecstatically, enriched by love and tender awareness. Both full and empty at the same time, the big mind descends upon the small self, erasing duality and self-inflicted boundaries.

The guest, the host, solitude and the marketplace, the suffering and all the joys of humankind sing a song of sweet reverence. Invisible lightning follows faithfully. Spaciousness, infinity. Upon the horizon, so much more.

The top of the head – a funnel embracing the skies. The body – an antennae for the unspeakable. "Talk to me," I encourage her, "in your own time." I know that she does not need my permission to do her work. An unseen smile on my lips, an invisible hand on my heart.

This silence is only to be surpassed by the silence of a purified heart. In this moment, right now, right here, the outer is recognized only by the true experience of the inner. Emptiness and spaciousness are the two opposing poles describing exactly the same thing.

"And now be quiet," she says, "and dissolve in the immensity."

# *Dissolve in This*

Dissolve in this, she said.

Drop after drop the divine nectar assembles in awe of its source. Above and below, the Aegean is dressed in myriad hues of blue. Bless your garments of dark and light.

A ripple arises as she holds me ever so tenderly. It gently washes over body and mind with a strong hand. The sands of time, sifted, rest upon the shore.

Wave after wave push against one another. So close and intimate in their essence, they embrace, give way and relax until the next movement arises.

Underneath all this the currents play hide and seek as tides come and go. Beyond the horizon, wind and temperature conduct the orchestra of spaciousness.

Flow with this, she says, as she rocks me gently from side to side. Salt and sun embalm both soul and skin, while all the liquids vibrate in perfect harmony.

Then stillness settles and it all begins anew.

# *Alone*

Love, she says, is the biggest threat. Arms and explosives are nothing compared to the invincibility of a purified heart. Yet you hold onto your poison as if it were your greatest treasure.

You are lost, she continues, entangled in the ways of the world. The colorful balloon of yourself is inflated to the maximum. Just a single pop will do. Let me help you out.

Her boat is safely moored in the ancient harbor as she extends her hand in my direction. Come into my world, she invites me, come and come now.

But there is hesitation on my part. Wait for me, I beg her silently, while I long for completion. Rummaging through my achievements, I can almost persuade myself, but not quite so.

Your mind is intoxicated by delusions, she affirms. Donate them to the winds and be free. I know that she is right in her assessment, but I just cannot let go just now.

Old habits of self-centeredness are recognized for what they are, before a new spontaneity of playfulness arises. Let's play together, my friend, she beckons with a smile.

My mind races through the same old circuitry in a perfectly conditioned brain. Is that really you, she asks me with a grin?

I don't know who I am.

All needs create unhealthy compromise, she maintains. Violating yourself and others creates regret for which you will never forgive yourself. Make a new beginning.

I fight for my life. All my strength is bound by what I think I am. Everything experienced both good and bad has me tied up in knots. There is no energy left for being in the present.

How can I convince myself of my own innocence when I know that my motives are ulterior ones? I love her and that love makes me despise her all the more.

On one hand I crave her approval while on the other I wish that she would sail away. She haunts me in my dreams and she awaits me so patiently wherever I go.

She speaks to me of a loss so great when all I want is to gain. My confidence, my self-esteem, my profits and my individuality are stripped before her surgical eyes.

I want to scream in agony. Don't talk to me like that. The words escape my throat, muffled for fear of being heard by the others. Don't visit me here again, I hiss. My tongue burns in my throat.

She does not meddle with my struggle, while her eyes seem to say a thousand words. They rest on my face with the calm steadiness of a mother watching her young at play.

I want, I say. I know, she answers. Forget yourself in this moment and hold nothing back. When you give everything, all is received.

Afraid to lose the little I have, my fists cling to the invisible with all my might. It is impossible to impress her, but I try ever so hard. I feel disqualified.

I wish she would stop right now. It is the hardest to hear something you already know from someone you love and hate at the same time.

She reminds me of my anger, my inert violence. But what can I do? It gnaws at my heart and eats at my soul. It shakes me. Showing it is out of the question. I lick my lips and rearrange my clothes instead.

Yes, my arrogance arises out of insecurity. My anger and hatred try to cover up the deep hurt inside this small heart of mine. I know that I am on the hook and there is no way to escape. This makes me furious.

Knowing her art well, I sense that she gives me some slack. Soon the line will tighten again, and the little freedom I gain will be short-lived. Inside my shawl I hide a threat of nervousness.

I will improve myself, I cry. She laughs and says: The reason why you don't see your true nature is because you always look in the wrong direction.

Projecting the arrow of attention outwards, it soon gets lost in space. When the momentum is spent you find yourself nowhere. Look in and all is revealed. It is so easy, dear.

Ecstasy is neither yours nor mine—it belongs to the Universe. Invite the Whole to dance through your limbs, to breathe through your pores, to celebrate whatever is in front of you.

Duality is my playground. It is safer that way. Business and pleasure, friendship and enmity rule my action. If I can sell your meat, the cleaver is my friend. If I cannot, you are.

Think with the stars, she reckons, consider it. See what they see from their transcendent point of view and realize that they embrace you as One of them. One of many.

How can I be one of them I wonder? I am better, I am more. I do whatever I want. I am the king of the Universe. I decide who lives and I decide who dies.

Surround yourself with an aura of benevolence, she tempts me. Let your feet massage the Earth, allow your hands to love whatever they touch. This place is your family.

She touches my chest with tenderness. Remember your heart, my dear. Look into the mirror and see your twisted face. Then, stop. Realize that all there is – is light.

Friendliness is the key to your own heart, she tells me. Open it without caution. Fear and guilty feeling have no place in my world. Trust, she says, and turns around.

As her sail straightens, my spirit dwindles. I see her on the horizon, unreachable, but all of this is just my imagination. In reality she is still right in front of me.

I hold onto my accomplishments. Oh how proud am I of my creation. I gesture to the stars above. Yes, she says, your toys are beautiful.

Success, my friend, she asserts, can be your worst enemy. Stay with your failures, acknowledge them openly and discover humility.

Humility, she continues, is the pathway to devotion. Devotion gives rise to emptiness. Suspended in emptiness the heart fills with over-flowing love for all that is.

Her wisdom disarms me for a moment, yet my defenses are well-trained and I lock my heart before I change my mind. It hurts too much to be vulnerable.

One final message of peace, she says, before she starts to go. But I don't listen anymore.

The seeds I sow in your heart, she declares (I find out later), will sprout and blossom in due time. In the garden of love the old crop of hurt and resentment makes space for the flowers of kindness and compassion.

With this she sails off into the infinite. On the beach, I am, alone.

# By the Pond

We sit by the pond and the wind plays with your hair. A solitary ripple breaks the silence of the quiet waters. The mountains, in the distance, watch without a whisper. The blue sky turns the water into heaven on Earth. Once again the pond is unstirred.

No one is here and the silence nourishes us with its richness.

For weeks I meet you everywhere I go. Your face is so familiar, and the softness of your voice calms my restless heart. I wonder where you come from and where you leave to so suddenly. It is always like this. You come and go like the wind.

Every time you disappear you take something away from me. I fear that one day you will not return, because there is nothing left to take.

# The Nameless

I hesitate to address you properly, while my heart is still securely moored in the ancient harbor. Maybe when the sails are set, the words will be spoken effortlessly.

Once upon a time, during the harvest season, you passed by my house oblivious to the village eyes. It was late that night, and the heat of the day mixed with the merciless labor had covered the villagers with a thick veil of dreamless sleep.

But I was absent on that occasion, and I don't even recall my destination. When I returned with the rising sun, my yesterdays had stayed behind. Now, even though I remember something, I don't know anything at all.

The neighbors were intoxicated by your fragrance for a while, mistaking it for mine. They asked what herbs I grow, and what momentous mixture is my delicious secret. I showed them your picture and suggested that they look you up.

They wondered about your whereabouts and how they may find you. I told them to look where they least expect your company—in the invisible breath and in the silent heartbeat.

Now that the winds have carried your fragrance to the other shore, I rejoice in silent anticipation. You know my ways and I know yours. We will meet again when I am truly absent.

# She Told Me

The last time we met, she told me about you – and her adoration for you made me shiver with joy. She is pure, and her heart beats in the rhythm of unconditional love. She lives the dream that most of us only imagine.

So, when she speaks, I fall silent ... and ... listen ... to the empty spaces that hide patiently between her words. She speaks of you with such veneration that I don't dare to entertain a single thought. And then ... what she tells of you ... becomes my own reality.

Her words move my heart beyond explanation and I wait and wait to hear her talk to me again. One day, I hope, I will be able to tell you all about her—in her own language of un- contaminated Silence...

# Your Finger on My Lips

I saw your face in the crowd one day, after the rain. The crisp air filled my heart with clarity and emptiness as the reeds stood in silence, still dripping. Your face was so familiar, yet I knew that it was the first time we had met. Still, tempted to greet you, you saw and put a cool finger on my lips. We held each other for a while, your heart upon mine, and I knew that the treasure would continue to grow on its own now.

When your form disappeared in the distance, I wanted to call you back. With every step you took, my heart cried out to you, but my lips remained sealed.

Now and then we meet again. My heart beats with yours, certain that it can't hold onto you for a single moment. We go our separate ways now, you and I, but I know that every step I take, I take with you.

And still your finger rests upon my lips...

# Tears

She cries her heart out every time I leave. But her tears are not made of acid and heartache – they are sweeter than honey. They wash the land of its past. Dust and dreams, impurities and pain are swallowed by the sea – her sister in arms. She knows that I never really leave. Where can I go without her?

Pines drop cones while oaks release acorns. The squirrels plant them for future generations knowing that we don't have as much of a future vision as nature does. Almonds and olives bow to the ground in gratitude while the tarmac glistens below. The atmosphere purified with clarity. Take off.

This is not the right time to be sad. The airlines are kind enough to allow me extra heart-luggage. She travels in style again, and, in good company. Love, compassion, bliss, truth and beauty caress her gently while she smiles the smile of forests and mountains, rivers and water-falls, beaches and whatever lies beyond.

I come and go, rest my head on her breasts and relax in her arms. There is nothing in her being that calculates or manipulates, nothing that looks for advantage, revenge, failure or success. Her openness welcomes all visitors with kindness and even her tears are the most delicious nectar for the one whose heart is ready – to love.

# The Art of Love

Incapable of the art of love

The heart complains

And an icy wind blows

In the abode of tender awareness

Tell me, friend, who knows love?

I have looked for many

And only found the One


Answers received in gratitude

Have only given birth

To a multitude of questions

Awakened from the dream

Illusion tries to hide

Its non-existent face

I am the One it cries, I am


But yet, you cannot fool

My love, my emptiness, for long

Awaken, heart, awaken now

For this eternal moment

When you are next to me, oblivious

You melt and then remember, once again

That you are One with everything


Tell me, heart

Where is your love, your tenderness

Your vulnerable solitude

Forget, remember, dream of me

And never speak as if

I am so far away from you

Your one and only friend, your attitude

# *Talk to Me*

Don't talk to me of love, until your heart has been purified by a Thousand Suns. Tell me of your pain and your misery, your longing and your failure. Once understood, your suffering will guide you aptly and is certain to shower you with the greatest blessings. Allow trust to arise. Don't try to hide your jealousy and your grief; make this a lesson in honesty. Show me where you lost your innocence, and then we can begin. Strip in front of me, until nothing is left unexposed.

Share with me what keeps you from celebrating your innermost nature. Take my hand and sing me a song that is entirely of your own melody and lyrics. If I hear you borrow a single note from another I will walk away from you.

Don't talk to me of silence, until your mind has been tranquilized by a Thousand Moons. Tell me of your confusion, your dreams and nightmares. When all illusions identify themselves as such, transcendence happens all by itself. There is nothing to do and nowhere to go. It is time to face the truth and stop projecting into the unforeseen. Be with me right here and right now and stop all mental activity.

Confide in me how your mind was twisted by envy and lust for power. Express your frustration at trying to be what you are not. Whisper how you lost the ability to think with the stars.

Don't smile at me unless both heart and mind have been transformed by night and day. Show me your tears and your anguish, your stress and your perplexity. But don't pretend ... because deceit masquerades not only the ugly but the beautiful as well.

Let me see your deepest wounds and let me hear your most distressing cries of agony. Look into my eyes and keep your gaze upon this emptiness until time has stopped and your suffering has vanished along with all that you think of as your sacred treasure. Drop your defenses unconditionally and be Silent – only then...

Talk to me of Love.

# The Merchant of Love

"Open your arms and offer your emptiness to me. It is nothing that I ask of you. Come as you are, no need to prepare yourself in any way. I am the merchant of love," she said.

"My business is unlike any other," she whispered. "I have nothing to sell, but everything to give. But only if you leave what you think you are, are you given the secret key."

"Consider yourself fortunate," she continued. "Not many are given this chance more than once. But this time know that you must come with empty hands and place all your cards face up."

"Hold nothing back," she sang joyfully, "and surrender so totally that your annihilation opens the sacred chamber. In your absence the empty space fills with unimaginable nectar."

"Now," she said with a grin and before she disappeared through the secret door, she repeated, "now you know all there is to know. Come when you are ready, come now."

# Freedom

Freedom, she said to me, is not to do what you want to do and when. Find liberation in open arms instead; blend one moment into another joyously.

Bask in the golden sunlight and take shelter under the cover of all-encompassing darkness. Stand in your own light and celebrate the protection of your own shadow.

Riding the waves, floating gently, going with the stream – abandoning plan, schedule and purpose. In this state of letting go, find liberation.

Flow with the winds and sway in the breeze. Let the currents take you to the center of motionlessness. Await the revelation in the face of the bountiful.

Let him who opens hearts be the master of all your endeavors. Compassion and servitude will guide you to be free when all else is bound and confined.

Forget yourself in modest celebration, she said. Be a waiting, and be an open invitation, a homage to this present moment.

# Say Yes

"Say Yes," she told me. "This," she said, "is the secret key to happiness."
"If it were so easy," I thought, "everyone would be in ecstasy." But then
I tried and tried and tried and found so many reasons to say – No. First
I said no to my body. I complained about my bad back and crooked
nose. My lacking endurance and the aches in both knees did not help
at all. But these were only my paltry overture.

"You want me to say Yes to this mess?" I asked her the next time
we met. "No," she replied, "no mess. Do you think God is an idiot and
you know better? What arrogance!" I never thought of it that way,"
I answered, and felt embarrassed. How interesting to look into my
artlessly woven web from a different vantage point. "You have acquired
some naughty habits," she said. "Nothing serious." With these words,
she vanished.

Hearing, not listening, I felt restless and disappointed and – stubborn-
ly proud of being out of tune with my body. If I would let it wilt and get
fat, I thought, I'd die of a heart attack. I took one last look at myself before
going to sleep. Couldn't persuade myself to give him a good night kiss:
"After all he is just a man," I thought, "and not very pretty."

Ahh, but I thought. I can do even better. With my body denied, my
mind was next. I hated every single thought in my brain. All my dreams
and desires, my memories, my past and my future chased each other
for the rest of the day. Perhaps I should admit myself to the mental
asylum, I thought. What is wrong with someone who thinks that he is
a toothbrush? This must be the arms of insanity.

That night, in dreams, all the sins of the past had a party, enjoying themselves in myriad ways. They awoke with me in the morning—as a feast of feats that now only left crumbs of regrets. She ran into me on the street, almost knocking me over. "I see you're all rattled," she said. "I am not as good as I always thought myself to be," I confided. "Rats," she replied, before she was gone with the wind. "Feed them and they will bring all their friends."

Perhaps, I thought, I would feel better if I could say no to my feelings too. I felt this and that. One moment fear, in another courage. Insecurity, now self-confidence. A fit of anger arose, arrogance appeared, sadness came and then left for a wave of joy to take its place. Am I out of my mind? Why yes, I thought. I left that behind yesterday…

As always, she was right. I felt guilty about beating myself up. Depression set in with a vengeance. I really did not like myself at all. Then what about love? "Saying yes," I thought, remembering her advice, "does not work for me. The birds in the park and the flowers in the meadow do not make a difference." Then jealousy arose – of those for whom it seemed so easy to be – themselves.

Now, "No" is my mantra. Pure magic, the answer to all the questions I ever had … as far back as I can remember. Myself, my work, my family, my hometown, my car, my house, my body and my mind are just not good enough. I want something that I never had. I long for love. "Well done, sweetheart," she whispers to me from nowhere. "Now that you know where you are, something can be done."

# Listen

Listen, my friend, she says, when I call your name. A mere whisper of the most familiar sound overrides the myriad voices of the Universe. In resonance with the flavor of vowels and consonants merged by an unseen hand, the cacophony of the World matures into a sweet melody of the Beyond.

Like a man who searches for the key in his pocket with one hand while he holds the object of desire in the other, arrest the momentum of the fleeting for a single moment. Stop and then be in tune with the heartbeat of the Absolute. Don't search, she says. Find.

## *You and You*

Once upon a time, when you were still you and I was still I, I looked deeply into your eyes, saying, "How beautiful you are."

Nowadays I don't see you anymore, even though the memories of the past tempt me with a benevolent gesture and a tender touch.

You have become a mirror to me: In your eyes I see myself and in your voice I hear my name.

But sometimes your proximity is too near and your distance seems too far away.

Then I long for the days when you were still you and I was still me.

# Good Morning

"Good morning," she says to me, as we rise above the lifting fog. The deep blue sky caresses our skin as we soar higher and higher. A fluffy cloud of dizziness arrests my attention for a while, before clarity envelops us in its velvet coat.

All you can see, she tells me, belongs to you. From below, you see but the little things. Carried by the absence of wanting, all there is ... is light.

As my eyes get used to the brightness, the landscape below becomes clearly visible. "Good morning," I reply to her, as we continue in her embrace.

It dawns upon my awakening that I can hold onto her only if I let her go. Then, to my surprise, I rise instead of fall. In this moment, below and above have one thing in common, and that is that they hold each other, close.

# Conversation

I felt her eyes on mine ever so gently, but I could not look at her the way my heart demanded it. It pounded and quivered, it raced and skipped from prairie to forest, from lush jungles to icy glaciers. Wherever I ventured she was there, looking straight into my soul.

Annihilation is a stake too high to bargain with: we prefer to show our beauty and our superiority. We like to prove our intelligence, and to reinstate our separate individuality. We cherish what we think of as ours and celebrate the differences.

What is the same falls through the cracks into oblivion.

Pretending to make good conversation, we laughed and joked and acted genuinely pleasant. I felt her presence close to mine, radiating with the heat of an invisible field. She was beautiful, I thought, strong and radiant, yet vulnerable and etheric. She was exactly what I was looking for.

Unacquainted with the tenderness between us the others were driven and consumed by their own agendas. Some shared and exchanged their merriment, while some thought one thing and said another. The art of love prefers to hide in the silent spaces, well in between one word and another.

For most it is a give and take of convenience, a symbiotic dance of the opposites. When I have what you lack and you offer what I need, we both smile and strike a deal. But business is conducted for gaining an advantage that in return is played at the right time—and we are then, even once more, ready for another conquest.

Her voice resounded deeply within my heart. "Don't give up on humanity." she said. "Don't give up on Love, my dear. Disappointment is a self-inflicted wound. Don't hurt yourself anymore." With that she reached for my hand, but I trembled and pretended not to notice.

Yet I felt her caress my fingers and the spaces in between what they thought they owned. Her hand was soft yet confident, her breath was so close that I could have sworn that it was my very own. For the longest time she just held me tight without saying a single word. Perhaps she did not think at all.

Thinking of it now, I guess that she did not want to make me feel uncomfortable in front of the others. Perhaps I would have misunderstood her along with them, and would have guessed what we always guess when love comes our way. She wants and demands what I am unable to give.

But had I looked into her heart another vista would have revealed its breathtaking beauty. She has no desire except to touch in the other what has been touched deep within her heart. Knowing that the queen of hearts deals her cards face up, she smiled. Once you know what you have got, there is no point in hiding it.

# You Must Leave Now

You must leave now. We stand by the mooring and choke back the tears that burn our hearts. No word can convey what our silence stirs in the depth of our souls. Our eyes meet briefly, and the sky sings its song of emptiness.

The provisions you loved so much seem childish to us now, so we left them behind. This time you must leave empty-handed.

The fog settles in the harbor, and by this time the others have returned and their ships resting peacefully, side by side. I want to tell you that every moment with you has been a great pleasure, but I know that if I do, you will turn and go. So I decide to stay with you, where it hurts the most.

I must leave now, wishing that your memory would remain with me, until I too go where you have gone today. But it is late in the evening, and dusk is rapidly descending. I try to hold the last image for a moment, and then I let you go. I turn around and walk back to the lonely village. The others are raising their glasses in salute to the One, while I walk alone.

Maybe someday, I will join them again.

# *You Are a Fool*

You are a fool to think that you can ever get away from me. Once I have laid my eyes upon you, I will haunt you forever and ever. Now that we have met, every flower on your path and every stone on the road will remind you of me. You will never be able to forget me, however hard you may try. Even in your dreams there is no escape.

I lurk in the first rays of the morning sun and in the shadows of the ancient oak. I am your husband and your wife, I am your mother and your child. Friend and enemy, my presence is always around you like a perfume of the beyond. I am all that you are and everything that you are not. You're hooked, my friend, she said to me.

When you run, you run from me, and when you come, you come to me. I am your future and your past, I am your present moment. Wherever you go you will find me, watching you. As long as you don't know me, you will feel safe. You think that it is you who takes the steps you do. But it is me tightening and then loosening the strings of your heart.

It will disturb you at first. It will make you toss and turn at night, it will soil your sheets with the sweat of fear and the tears of agony. It will make you want to shed your mortal coil, just to get away from me. But I warn you in advance. It is I who gives you life and it is I who takes it away again. Be with me from now on and stop quarreling.

# The Friend

Perhaps I ought to listen to the friend who advised that when loneliness is all around, surround yourself with lovers only—the others just want to sell you something.

A lovely girl crossed my favorite path that day, a sweetheart and a beauty, too. She came to sell her love, but her price was too high. She wanted less than my life—I got away to save myself. The only death worth dying for is in the arms of unconditional love.

An author of clever books set out to convince me with his words of wisdom. In between the articulate lines his actions and the twisted heart of pretension left a bitter taste in my mouth. It is sweetness that I long for.

A young man I worked with offered me his enmity. I loved him for his strength and for the depth of his voice, but declined his gracious offer. No one else can lift what is heavy upon your own heart.

A business man desiring to secure a project lured me with his grand success but kept his failures hidden deep within. Come back, I told him, when you are ready to share everything.

A housewife on her way home hawked her timid loneliness. The string of words she pronounced anesthetized the senses, as she begged, "Hold me tenderly and never let me go. Don't speak, just look into my eyes, and ... be." I couldn't stay and said goodbye.

A famous artist tried to sell me his colorful paintings, but refused to paint in his own blood. What kind of art is this, I wondered, that does not touch the soul with the very stuff that it is made of?

A politician campaigning in my town wanted to sell his lies. Tempted as I was to believe in his good intentions (for my own reasons), I turned down the unethical. Pretending not to know is much worse than ignorance.

A drifting prostitute asked me to buy her body for a good price. Her curves seduced my mind but left me broken-hearted and blue. Her heart was sweet but her love was but a small fragment of the heavenly mosaic.

An athlete in the park wanted to part with his strength. How lovely the orchestra of muscles and tendons, of bones and connective tissue played in harmony, yet his softness was not on the market, and I, declined.

A beggar scrimping for food proposed to barter his poverty, yet I could not make any of that my own. Though I shared some of his paralyzing fears and he partook in the wildest of my dreams, we walked away in opposite directions.

A musician loved by many invited me to purchase his song. His melody was quite delicious; still his rhythm lacked the untamed character of freedom. It is in the absence of restriction that liberation begins its spontaneous dance.

An arrogant professor surrounded by his air of confidence wanted to impress me with his knowledge. His brain brimming with borrowed substance, he was an unhappy man. I enquired: What can you teach me that you have not learned yourself?

A creative architect in a sterile office recommended his expertise in structure. Whatever was straight in him had been bent by the logic of for and against. He missed the nectar of playfulness in his actions, and left me shaking his head.

A retired engineer squeezed me into the mechanical brace of life. It jammed the fragile wings of creativity and reminded me of a bird caged in the middle of the forest. A tear shed, a sharp pain and I was gone.

A tailor dressed me in his cotton quite certain to bring out the best in me. But then free spirit struggled, broke away and soared into the deep blue skies—clouds caressing his veins, wind blowing the restrictions out of his skin—and I left the tailor quite joyfully.

A salesman played upon my greed with a useless product. He charmed me with all the tricks of the trade, praying upon the hurts of the past and the dreams of an anticipated future. Tied to the present by the rope of awareness, I returned to the present.

A child bumped into me as I mused about the meetings of the day. Excuse me, sir, he yelled, already half way around the corner. Finally, I thought, there is someone who wants nothing from me at all, not even a reply.

I told the friend and he replied, "Joy leads to suffering and pleasure turns into pain; mobility is the sister of inaction while bliss is the brother of misery. Tell me who is able to give you one hundred percent?"

"Don't waste your time, my friend," he said, "and never accept less than the Universe itself. Whatever you bargain for, you pay for with your heart, your soul, your vulnerability. You pay for it with the heartbeat of your very life.

"Surround yourself with lovers only," he advised, while he walked away, slowly. He knew that I would cherish every word he said.

# *Tender Persuasion*

She always lets me know when she is around, in her mysterious ways. There is no mistaking her presence for another. I can't say that I miss her, because it is her silent whisper coming through my lips. The tenderness of her voice makes my heart burst into a thousand flames. In the glowing embers all shivering comes to an end. It is her warmth that fills my heart with intoxicating sweetness.

Wanting her, she steals away unnoticed. Her visits must always be a surprise. Her terms are simple, her demeanor pure delight. She longs for light and offers you fire. She thrives on love and opens your heart. She feeds on silence and gives you pure consciousness.

A flicker of love lighting a busy moment tells her story. Like a thief in the night, she enters my house when all visitors have left. The doors of the senses are her usual access route, but a simple knowing or a silent recognition will do. She knows that I crave the intimacy of her embrace and the tenderness of her silken touch. There is no need to talk – we have said it all. Her proximity is the answer to my deepest longing.

Lost in the ways of the world, her voice goes unheard. It is not that she hides it purposely. She does not want to be looked for, she wants to be found. She is not fond of the miserable but is always in favor of the celebration. In her arms the inner vision becomes a reality.

A familiar fragrance alerts me to her presence. It sharpens the avenues of perception with the breath of kindness. Whether we know it or not we all work in her service. She tightens the strings of the heart with perfect tension. She strums any instrument in the rhythm of the unknown. What resonates, heals; what falls in tune, brings harmony. Her voice transforms day-to-day confusion into delicious clarity.

Truth, beauty and bliss are her playground. She swings on the open wings of laughter. She slides on the deep slopes of the authentic. She talks to the essence of all things. All the while, her ecstatic expression has no motive whatsoever. A single glimpse is enough for a life of Awakening.

A quaint rustle in the reeds announces her closeness. Her timing is impeccable as usual. She lures me into the ordinary without tempting promises. I follow her wherever she goes. Her companionship is the antidote to boredom. She leads me out of my comfort zone quite certain that I won't resist. Stripped of desire and achievement, we laugh at my sheepishness.

She beckons with closeness and teases with distance. She calls out loud, then falls silent. She tickles the soul and laughs at her own jokes. Despair and frustration are foreign to her playfulness. Any opportunity is just good enough. She never holds back and never gives up on us.

The smile on an unknown face suggests that she is near. She is the master of disguise, the queen of persuasion. She silently slips into a multitude of roles—be they form or formless, sentient or solid rock, whatever is placed in front of her, she enlivens the living and reanimates the dead. In her company, heartache and agony, fear and suffering are forgotten. Without her, you and I would not be here at all.

# *Precious*

Invisible by nature you slip into every moment so naturally. It is you who speaks through pleasure and pain, through tears and laughter. Unaware and profoundly intoxicated by our preferences, we take the perfume of the moment for life itself, sometimes sour – sometimes sweet.

I am so shy to tell you, my love, that we forget you most of the time and that we remember you only in times of great despair. It hurts to talk to you like this and I know that the only antidote for our habitual failure is gratitude and appreciation of this moment. Precious you are, my love, so precious...

# *Precious Love*

You tell me that you are my prison and my liberation. I tell you that am your beggar and your king. I am free to go within your garden, but at the gate I turn and look the other way. It belongs to the past, to the days of pain and suffering.

You shower me with your flowers and wash my feet with precious perfume. You guide me when no one else is prepared to restrain my passionate nature. I sit on your throne and rule the four corners of your kingdom with love and compassion.

The seeds you sow in my heart are meant to grow protected by warm and velvety darkness. Don't consider what will become of them. Like you and like me they too follow their own path. Their destiny is unknown, their future is uncertain.

You take my hand and I hold you with utmost devotion. Your flowering is my only real concern, knowing that our scents will produce the fragrance of transcendence. Precious love, a single step will do.

# Live Your Life

Live your life, my friend, she said. The poetry of this moment wants to be read out loud by you. Each syllable holds a secret key for silent enjoyment. Word by word the world unfolds in your presence. Hand in hand the sentences embrace the wholeness of the Universe. From the first chapter to the last the boundaries of duality are dismantled tenderly.

Embrace this wondrousness. Grateful, yet without attachment let it all pass through you. The elements are your friends and the seasons are your trusted allies. Nothing experienced is forever, everything within you and without you is a playful flow. Touch, caress, but don't hold on. Benediction showers upon you in saturation, not in ownership.

Allow the flame of love to ignite your heart. Let it consume all that is impure and unessential. Burn and give light to those around you. Stand tall and forget yourself. See life pulsate and reveal itself in thoughts and actions and lift this moment to the heavens. Then tell me what it is like to be here. Before that, devote yourself to nothingness and just stay quiet.

# *The Mirror*

Doing nothing in particular is your splendid art. Your genius of aesthetic perfection is steeped in the secret of absence. This is your action, your playful skill: You resonate with what is placed in front of you.

Sometimes you show me what I want to see. My dreams and aspirations are grasping for emptiness with hands so full of longing. Most secret fantasies circle around how I want to be. Imagination is forever in the distant future, a mirage of light.

You encourage me to face what I fear the most. Trembling,

I turn to look as far away as possible. But you never let me get away with the act of straying in delusion and always remind me of the present moment. It is here and now that we find – love.

Still young, I try to mimic your behavior: I stand and walk as you do. Then, I hear you laugh about the absurdity of one trying to be – another. Okay, you say, let's dance, but invent your own choreography.

At times you kindly point me towards the other side of things.

The ultimate reality plays hide and seek in a spoke frozen in the wheel of time. A tiny grain of sand becomes aware of this celestial body, a part rejoicing with the Whole.

Grateful to be here we celebrate a moment of ecstasy. Catching us by surprise we ride a delightful wave of bliss from this moment into the next. A flicker of enlightenment erases the darkness that still lurks behind it.

From the hidden side you acquaint me with a beautiful detail of an ancient statue. Marble cliffs polished by the gentleness of the sea for Millennia. The classical nose gives away the strength of perfect confidence heightened by childlike innocence.

Sunlight, integrity and honesty dazzle my eyes in the morning.

Still not quite awakened, I mumble, "Let me sleep – a little longer." Your compassion, so delicious, pierces the veil of yet the sweetest dream.

You introduce me to nothing special—appreciation of the simple things. As a step forward enters new territory, the gravel leaves an imprint on the sole of the foot for a little while. The deep blue sky reflects itself in you without effort.

This empty moment overwhelms my soul. In spaciousness, my laughter, my tears and my silence find themselves at home so joyfully. Contagiously, you smile ... you whisper, "My friend, awaken, wake up now. You still have some more loving to do, today."

# Longing

"When you dream of something," she said to me, "your desire is born out of feeling incomplete or perhaps inadequate. By fulfilling your desires, you anticipate that the underlying deficiency will be erased and that you will feel whole and, in your own sense, perfect. But this perfection can never be reached by any outer means; it can only be understood from deep within."

All your life you have come to me with your worldly desires, thinking that you will find happiness when you reach this or that. And now you think that I am here to grant you the ultimate desire.

You want enlightenment, hoping that enlightenment means the end of your misery. But if you birth this desire without loving yourself as you are, it is just another birth of the ego.

Instead of making yet another projection into the future that will never come to be, go ahead and nurture Longing. Longing awakens out of remembrance. Your nature is not something that you must attain. It is your one and only natural development. You can neither achieve it nor miss it; you can neither force it nor postpone it.

"So now," she said, "relax, until all the strings of your heart and mind are tuned just right, and then…"

# The Longing

Heart needs warmth

Give it Love

Make (infinite) space

Let it Fill


Be patient

Relax into being

Enjoy trust

Know what's right


Mind strives for clarity

Stop thoughts

Maintain stillness

Forget everything


Learn discipline

Stay focused

Be positive

Break patterns

Fire wants fuel

Offer your Self

Light the flame

Watch it burn

Have faith

Honor truth

Think big

Look beyond


Life demands awareness

Be Present

Step aside

Celebrate your Soul


Breathe deeply

Remain silent

Love well

Live each moment


Dream longs for awakening

Wake up

Gather courage

Step into the Light


Enjoy what you are

Long for what is

Cherish the moment

Be here

# Not What You Say

It is not what you say to me but rather what you don't. Your silence speaks straight to my heart as the clouds settle and the morning dew washes the night away. Stop searching now, you seem to say, and, don't ask any more. Your restless eyes swallow the unseen and your questions raise the fog beyond the known. This is where pain and suffering begin, and this is where it all ends.

It is not what you do to me but rather what you don't. Your stillness shakes me to my roots, as the sun rises and the open sky stretches from there to here. Don't lose yourself in action, you seem to say, and let it all happen by itself. Your automatic movement twists the formless and your will falls for its own imagination.

This is the moment you have been waiting for, and this is the moment that never comes.

# I Worship You

Of all the Ones I know, and those I haven't met ... I worship You. Deep in my heart, away from the chatter of the world, there is a sacred chamber just for You. You and only You may come and go as you please, while the others stay outside awaiting invitation.

Sometimes, I am hard on you, while the others enjoy my overwhelming tenderness. The generous leeway I extend to them – stops at your doorstep. But this, this is the cruel rule of Oneness: The Ocean of Love drowns the One and the Many, and this is here exclusively – for You.

# Missing You

I miss you, my love, as if a Million years of solitude sprawl out their spaciousness in between us. A silent breath and a lonely heartbeat scream out in unison: You are not here! Sweet tears burn heart-shaped holes into my open chest—they know how to reach the innermost core.

Your love is the nectar of my soul. Without it not a moment of life is worth living; yet with it, the stars shower the blessings of the beyond upon my loneliness.

It is so dark tonight. An icicle of fear grips my heart with its frozen fingers. But in the darkest night, the stars shine ever so brightly and the intensity of the cold goes by unnoticed – your love is my destiny.

I long for you, my love. I lay awake for hours, searching for you in all the corners of the Universe. Where can you be now? Have you forsaken me, or is it me who has lost himself in a maze of desire? A gentle rain washes my dreams away, just before dawn.

Your heartbeat and mine are fused with the timelessness of eternity. Still I wonder if you will ever return to me; who am I in the depth of your eyes?

Your favorite wine and the rhythm of my heart will guard you at the door. Will their longing be in vain, or will your sweet love fill their emptiness once again? I for one will never know...

Where are you, my love? Did you follow the call that was meant for our awakening? Did you have a choice, or were you just like me ... a leaf in the autumn wind...

I will wait at the waterfront, another day, scanning the ocean. The horizon (far today) will remain far tomorrow. What will the new day bring: liberation or despair?

You may think that your departure will ignite my heart until the end of time. But I must tell you that it is past time for the newness of that thought. My fate was sealed the moment I first laid eyes on you. You are my destiny ... my departure and my arrival. You are the harbor that shelters my ship and the storm that destroys it, mercilessly.

I am yours, my love. You know that my heart belongs to you and that every breath I take, I take with you. I cannot take a single step without you, for one step leads to another and another one can only be had with you.

I love you endlessly and in that love lies a promise made a thousand years ago: I will find you and rest in your presence until the end of time ... come what may.

# Free Falling

Trust, she says. Surrender your life into the hands of the Almighty. Give up all hope of a better future, and abandon the notion of the small self. Embraced by the eyes of the infinite, enter the realm of innocence. The boundless freedom of not knowing dissolves the contamination of ignorance.

Like a skydiver riding the unseen currents of the ether, or a surfer on top of the seventh wave, renounce the veil that hides the ultimate reality. Abundance, she says, is when everything is good enough as it is... happiness is. While misery is the continuation of becoming.

Stunned by the flexibility of her mysterious wisdom, the present moment opens up onto an eternal vista of absence. Silence descends upon the perpetual activity of the mind and leaves me suspended in a pulsating and silent orchestra of an ever-expanding vacuum. This, she says. And then vanishes, suddenly.

# Surrender

Surrender your suffering to me, she said. I don't care for your riches or your victories. Your praise and your criticism are meaningless to me. In my world admiration and deceit are one and the same.

Let me caress your soul with the balsam of sweetness. As the dark spots lighten and unite with the luminous, the singular evaporates in the common pool drop by drop. Brilliance never struggles with the dark forces.

Stretch your imagination to the limit, then loosen up and relax. The inevitable awaits your arrival patiently no matter what you do. Give me everything that you don't have and gain what is yours to keep.

Allow me to pluck the strings of your heart with the sound of my voice. It hides as an undertone of the mundane and as the overture of the obvious. The orchestra of harmony is forever conducted by your own hand.

# More Tears

I cry for you, my Love, because


We beat you with ignorance

We punish you with greed

We curse you in your own name

We crush you with self-centeredness

We twist you with ulterior motives

We manipulate you with jealousy

We strangle you with hatred

We stab you with maliciousness

We sabotage you with aggression

We violate you by hurting ourselves

We damage you with anger

We suffocate you with shame

We defile you with prejudice

We torture you with bitterness

We wound you with delusion

We scar you with shame

We tear you with doubt

We cut you with irritation

We bruise you with cowardice

We execute you with fury

We harm you with frustration

We abuse you with deceit

We injure you with grief

We choke you with agony

We impair you with anguish

We hit you with bitterness


We pretend that we know better than you do, and still you caress us again and again.


In your name


we kill and hurt

we wound and injure

we rape and rob

we steal and murder

we lie and cheat

we abuse and control

we hate and demand

we shame and break

we dominate and judge

we complain and condemn

We sabotage and fear

we blackmail and control

we damage and harass

we punish and ridicule

we scare and terrify

We criticize and humiliate

we insult and manipulate

we blame and bully

we hate and insult

we abandon and reject

we mock and attack

we molest and provoke

we blame and intimidate

we neglect and disrespect


Looking for you

we succeed and fail

we get well and get sick

we are born and we die

we grow old and stay young

We eat, pray and meditate

we fast and binge

we get promoted and lose our jobs

We get married and divorced

we procreate, we remain celibate

We abuse drugs and lead a pious life

We breathe and fart

and do everything in between the two

We do everything for you


I cry for you, my Love.

# I Dream of You Today

I dream of you today. In front of my inner eye, I see how you clothe me in the finest garments. I see the love in your eyes as I hear you call my name. And then all is silent. When I have finally found you, you walk away from me.

I dream of you today. The cries of the night birds tell me that you are near. I listen to your voice like a child longing for its mother. When you come close to me, and your breath touches my open heart, I shrivel up and go astray.

I dream of you today. I feel your caress and see your smile, yet I miss you and long for something else. What this may be, I wonder, carelessly. I gamble away your treasures as you let me sit with mine.

I dream of you today and realize that my desires keep you away from me. The sound of my voice scares your messengers and my footsteps disturb the peace of your environs. Stop interfering, you tell me, as I listen.

I dream of you today. I hear your words and listen to the Silence. The emptiness in between the words carries your message to my heart. Resist, you tell me, and you are bound in suffering forever.

I dream of you today

# *The Hill*

On Vigla hill I run into an old friend. A warm embrace and a few joyful steps later we sit on the cliff overlooking the bay. She always appears at the right time. It is quiet here off-season except for the wind, the waves and the captivating silence. Most visitors escape from the island during the winter for that reason. The ancient harbor below, the big sky above, we find ourselves just in the middle.

Love, she says to me, is a jealous mistress; never bargain with her. Sometimes she tempts you with the scent of attraction; another time she feeds upon your loneliness. She may charm you with reason, or woo you with convenience. But when she comes your way without a motive, my friend, surrender. Her hands in mine are soft and tender, yet irresistibly strong. I know that I can never let her go.

Just like me, the seabirds have left their home for an excursion. It is too stormy out there. On the horizon, large waves dance to a hypnotic rhythm that does not reach this far. We can only guess. Down below us the waves caress the shore ever so playfully. They remind me of her, as she turns to me and speaks. Never take her for granted, she says, place all your cards on the table. Strategy belongs to the art of war.

I know where to find her. Love comes to your door by invitation only, she continues. Don't embarrass me with stinginess. Are you ready to give it all and everything? There is a price on your head, she confides in me. I wonder what the villagers thought of her when she was young? Her breath- taking beauty, the intensity of her demeanor, the intoxication of her presence must have attracted love and jealousy.

Don't try to escape now, she continues. Be courageous, my friend. Your fears and feelings of inadequacy are an extravagance you cannot afford. What is keeping you from finding your heart's desire? Invite her, she says, say yes and then forget and wait patiently. The whole hill is covered in pieces of ceramics of all sizes. Broken vessels, broken vows. A mountain of promises given but never retrieved.

What can you say to someone who speaks the language of love? You cringe and quiver, you shrink and expand, you laugh and cry, you fall into despair, you are shaken by waves of bliss. The Genovese ruins above witness both happy and challenging moments patiently. Looking out towards the islands of Chios and Psara, they see the beauty day in and day out, but they will never reach it.

When you have found love, she envisions, the work begins. Feed the fire with dry wood, cherish the flame with ample oxygen. Love, she says, needs awareness and attention. At the point of annihilation, continue. Clouds gather and disperse, shyness and conceit dance across the sky, just before the first drops fall. The land is washed of all impurities. Picking myself up, I notice that she is gone, until we meet again.

# Sit With Your Soul

Sit with your soul, brother, when your busyness has flooded your world with delusions, and let it teach you the ways of the Sun. Let it scorch the barren fields of jealousy with the rays of illumination. Allow it to dry out the swampland of illusion with the light of awareness. Request it to ignite the iron fetters of ignorance. Welcome it to burn up the stiff boundaries of selfishness. Encourage it to bring luminance to the dark foreboding corners of the unknown. Entice it to melt the hard shell of the grossness that surrounds it. And then, in the end, invite it to pervade your being with compassion.

Sit with your soul, sister, when the weight of the world weighs too heavily on your back and let it teach you the ways of the Moon. Say goodbye to the debilitating desire to be loved, with gratitude. Forget the inbred identification with the beauty of your youth and embrace the intoxication of the moment. Refuse the restraining notion of having space rather than giving it – to everything. Realize that knowing and not knowing awaken effortlessly in absence, when clouds have covered it, regardless. Know that silken darkness encompasses all that is with equal measure, right now. And then, in the end, kiss the mirror, with passion.

Sit with your soul, sisters and brothers, and let it teach you the ways of the Universe. Sun and Moon hold hands at dawn and dusk with the eternal promise to nourish both day and night. Unlock your inner sky to request the rise and fall of the planets and see that this – your nature – is the abode of the Universe. A single frame extracted from the grip of time is enough to understand and be transformed. But it may take time to develop a positive habit of sitting with your soul, sister and brother, holding hands and merging the opposites in the vast inner space of your awakening heart.

Sit with your soul and be, that.

# Gánga

Sat by the river with an old friend today. In action and in stillness the waters whisper ever so sweetly. Hiding under a dry leaf, a baby frog awaits his evening meal, emerged in blissful patience. It is not difficult to wait for eternity. She is always right here within reach.

We have not seen each other for years. Many friends have come and gone. Some have gone downstream, others like us are resting by the shore, still admiring the daily miracle. A refreshing cup of tea and a delightful smile later, the river begins to speak.

My friends, she says, you are my guests, my witness, my angels and my heritage. Sit quietly, watch attentively and speak from the heart. Tell my story, share my wisdom, quench the thirst of those who come from the mountains. Be my lips, my voice – but never forget, that.

We understand the ways of the water well.

It is time to part, she says, but both of us know that departure and arrival are but a single dot in the company of the Milky Way. Each step only leads to itself. We hug and kiss and wave and know – it is so good to be here.

# *Speaking of You*

I speak of you to my friends
But I hesitate to introduce them to you
In person

I fear that they will not know you
When they look into your eyes
And that they will miss the beauty of your silence

I worry that they may be oblivious
Of your all-encompassing presence
As they continue raving about your heavenly virtues

But this is theirs and yours is mine
I think of you all day and all night
I remember you in my words and in the silence in between

I clothe your image in everything I do
While you bless me with your stillness
And speak of me, saying nothing at all

Maybe, one day
I will speak of you
The same way

# Ecstasy

The formless council has assembled on your behalf innumerable times. Infinite wisdom dressed you in the brocaded garments of Kings and Queens, as well as the tattered rags of beggars and slaves. Sinner and saint, you are everything, she said. You are the World.

I see no ecstasy in your face, my friend. Where is the lightness of the air, the solidity of the earth, the all-consuming heat of fire? What about the liquidity of water, and the etheric flow of the invisible? You say that you follow the natural way and pursue the example of the great master.

Still your heart is governed by fear and your mind is deluded by the collective suffering of mankind. Mistaking this as your own, you focus upon the superficial while leaving the blissful essence unseen. Wake up, my friend, she said, and find love in the small things.

Listen to your teachers attentively:

Talk to the birds who show you how to fly

Touch the fields that provide growth for every living thing Listen to the secrets of the flames who transform the base into the subtle

Taste the ocean and quench the thirst of infinity

Sense the silence in between all actions.

You think that you are superior and you look at your neighbor with contempt. It is the simple man who builds the world and gives his life for a future that he will never see. Your mind is filled with great ideas, but you do nothing. Discover the art of service and make your world a revelation of beauty.

Perform the dance of life joyously. There is but a single chance in each moment. Dissolve in the nectar of sweetness that always surrounds you. Expand in the vastness of silence and fill the Universe with simple presence. Let all the stars shine and cast light and shadow upon you.

Return to innocence, remember your name, and my company...

# *Leela*

Let's play, my friend, she said, that life is a game. Let me introduce you to my team. She playfully pokes me in between the fifth and sixth ribs, as is her habit when she wants to make a point. Nudging this particular body part, she knows that she can hurt me just enough to get the message, but not enough to complain.

We have goalkeepers and goal getters, she continues. We have those who give it all they've got and those whose greatest merit is their laziness. Their positions vary greatly. While all are ambitious enough to fulfill their potential only some of them can commit to being coached. I take them all under my wings playfully.

Don't be so serious, my friend, she says. I'll let you in on my secret: I run both teams, for and against, but they don't know it yet. Each one thinks that this game is about competing, while I laugh and cry knowing that one single team can never play by itself.

The beauty of my game, she continues, is that there is a place for everyone. We need those who excel, as well as those who are a lost cause to themselves. We need the arrogant and the modest, the happy and the miserable. What role are you going to play today?

You must know that I juggle my teams anew each day: so don't dare to think that your position will be one and the same for the whole season. It is not even the same in an afternoon.

On both sides we have defenders, midfielders and attackers. We have those whose sole purpose is to block and others that are here to carry the torch for future generations.

You will break your head if you continue like that, she tells me, giggling, while I still try to hold onto my own rules. She wipes her hand across the sand casually, erasing our game with a few strokes. My pieces and hers lose their identity in a flash. Let's start anew, she says with a grin. Life is just a game!

# Going Up and Coming Down

Going up is great but only after you come down from the peaks can you share what has been experienced with others. A present becomes what it is meant to be only after it is given.

As you enter the gate the tigers whisper in your ears: "From the beginning to the end." This includes everything, and nothing is left out. No need to fear the beasts for their diet is your restriction. They devour your conditions and your hesitation. They chew your insecurity and your lack of trust. They absorb your fear and lick their chops in anticipation. You enter the gate, naked.

Her greeting is a reminder. "Listen," she says. "My love, my heart and yours beat in the same rhythm."

"Listen," she says, "as you hear the sound of each droplet filling your cupped hands."

You drink as she raises her voice once more.

"Remember," she says. "Remember your promise today." With this she releases you into freedom.

Attached by a thin thread to your hands, the Buddha smiles. Do you feel that smile upon your own lips? Does his emptiness pervade your being gracefully? Is the Buddha in front of you? Behind you? Inside you?

The answer is simple, but it can never be said. As you break the Silence, the secret is forgotten.

You think that it is beautiful up here, but this beauty is really your very own. Where Heaven and Earth meet you find yourself. This is the moment where life begins. Before Satori life is just a thick wad of fog burning away in the first rays of the new morning. Now you begin to be human. Get up and walk on.

An infinite number of trees make a forest, numerable houses make a village, enough women, their men and their children make humanity. Together we make the world. Where did you get the idea of your separate identity? Let your hardness melt in front of the ancient cedar. As liquid, enter the stream of life and be everywhere. And now let the nectar pulsate with love.

Coming down again purifies the heart while it frees the mind of its imaginary achievements. Self-realization is a nectar not hard to extract; all else is stalk and chaff. A rose is always a rose – the last steps are taken with utmost humility. You are back on Earth ... now make something good of your life.

# The Natural Forces

My friend, she says, pay attention to the natural forces.

Son and daughter, mother and father unite the Universe. Encompassing the cosmic ocean these words embody love and compassion. They point towards surrender and devotion. Without intention they carry the unforgettable fragrance of oneness.

Your parents and your children, she says, hold the secret key. Talk to each other, communicate. Work out conflicts in the present moment.

Biological conscience manifests in potentialities: there is an option for this or that. Alongside the path to freedom you find the left turn and the right curve of choice. On the unfolding circle of life, direction has no ultimate significance. You get there, anyway.

Whatever you do, she says, do it joyfully. Forget gain and profit—just do things for their own sake.

Instead of following the natural flow of what we came here for, we prefer to resist. We desire what we don't have, and find fault with who and what we are. Selfishness is a blindfolded guide. Thank god that we can't have it our own way.

Trust in the wisdom of the beyond, my friend, she says. The small self is an illusion, discard it, now.

Deep within the body hibernate the healing forces of the galaxies. Gases and minerals mix, combine and separate to give shape to the formless. Skin and bone, cartilage and tissue, organs and ever-flowing liquid are the manifestation of timeless wisdom.

Allow the celestial ambrosia to spread and work freely, she says. Say it, and it will be done.

The eternal game of action and rest, of well-being and detoxification is not in tune with our ephemeral quest for pleasure. Challenged by expectation and discontent, disturbed by age and discomfort, we forget the body's very own natural rhythm.

Don't step, she says. Dance. Tune into the pulse of the natural forces and give yourself fully.

Nothing can exist by itself. Heart-mind and body, earth, moon, and sun, planets and stars are irrefutably one. There is no constant in the Universe except for unimaginable spaciousness. In this divine playground the gods play the game of change. Stillness and activity caress each other tenderly.

Wake up, my friend, she says. This is your time – now.

# *Full Circle*

Unbelievable blissful darkness within and without

Stretching growing limbs and tissue

Expanding ancient consciousness

Floating in all-encompassing Oneness


The canvas clear, pulsating with life

Unknown beauty longing to express itself

In new ways each and every time

The daily miracle unfolds witnessed by infinity


Conceived and born out of love

Liquid spirit solidifies as mind and body fuse

Who will he be, what will she create

Images form thought, mind becomes action


Night and day embrace each other playfully

Happiness and suffering dance to their own rhythm

Innocence fades and becomes twisted character

Illusion disperses clarity, fog arises, thickens

A multitude of mirrors contort reality

The little self so proud and self-centered

Narrow-minded man so miserable all by himself

Lonely and heart-broken, the pot boils over


Personal pronouns lost in thought-torture

Identity confused in overwhelming plenitude

The essence lost in its very own vastness

Stunned into contentment, hit by lightning


The un-expectable wakeup call

You are all of this, she said, and nothing

Unbelievable blissful darkness within and without

Know yourself as light.

# *Epilogue*

Dear Friend,

Thank you for having read this book. Perhaps you are now considering giving it to someone you love as a present. The last few pages were left blank as an invitation for you to write a love letter in your own hand.

Write to your beloved, your parent or your child, a friend or someone yet unknown, whose heart is longing to unite with yours but has not yet found a way to do so. Or perhaps write this love letter to yourself.

Fall in love with the love in your heart and allow it to spread to the far corners of the Universe, then let the inspiration arise in its own time and put your love into action... enjoy.

Your Friend,

Frank Arjava Petter

If you would like to get in touch with the author, please find him at www.FrankArjavaPetter.com, follow him on Facebook and Instagram, send him an email at: FrankArjavaPetter@gmail.com, or find him in beautiful Eressos on Lesvos Island, Greece.

.

Printed in Poland
by Amazon Fulfillment
Poland Sp. z o.o., Wrocław

83199135R10074